Jurassic Bark!

By Hollis James
Illustrated by Fabrizio Petrossi

A GOLDEN BOOK • NEW YORK

© 2017 Spin Master PAW Productions Inc. All rights reserved. Published in the United States by Golden Books, an imprint of Random House Children's Books, a division of Penguin Random House LLC, 1745 Broadway, New York, NY 10019, and in Canada by Penguin Random House Canada Limited, Toronto. Golden Books, A Golden Book, A Little Golden Book, the G colophon, and the distinctive gold spine are registered trademarks of Penguin Random House LLC. PAW Patrol and all related titles, logos, and characters are trademarks of Spin Master Ltd. Nickelodeon and all related titles and logos are trademarks of Viacom International Inc.
T#: 488922
randomhousekids.com
ISBN 978-0-399-55880-1
Printed in the United States of America
10 9 8 7 6 5 4 3

It was an exciting day for the PAW Patrol. They were going on a hunt for dinosaur bones!

"Are you pup paleontologists primed for a big dino dig?" asked Cap'n Turbot.

"I'm ready to shovel!" said Rubble. "We want to find fossils—bones that are so old, they're hard as rocks," Ryder said.

The PAW Patroller rolled up to the dig site, and the pups went to work.

While Chase placed traffic cones to keep the work area safe, Rubble used his shovel to dig.

"Whoa! My shovel hit something!" exclaimed Rubble.

Cap'n Turbot was amazed at what Rubble had found. "These are a billion times better than dino bones—they're dino *eggs*!"

"Way to dig, Rubble!" said Ryder.

Marshall used his X-ray to look inside the eggs. "You definitely made a dandy discovery for the museum's diorama," said Cap'n Turbot.

Later, the pups tried to guess what was inside the eggs.

"I bet they're pterodactyls," said Marshall.

"Or *pup*-odactyls!" added Skye.

But Rubble was tired from his big day of digging. "Time for a prehistoric nap," he said, and his head filled with dinosaurs as he began to dream. . . .

Dinosaurs were everywhere in Adventure Bay! A mother pterodactyl built a nest for her three eggs, but one rolled out and landed in a tree.

A triceratops and her child wandered the hills.

And a giant Utahraptor ate Mayor Goodway's lunch!

Rubble was about to rescue the pterodactyl egg in the tree when suddenly, it hatched! The other eggs in the nest hatched, too! Three small flying dinos zoomed into the air.

Rubble had no time to save the pterodactyls because a train was having trouble with a triceratops!

Rubble sped to the stopped
train and found a baby triceratops
resting on the tracks in front of it.
"Triceratops are my favorite
dinos!" said Rubble. "Let's get you
off the tracks!"

Rubble climbed onto the triceratops's back, and the dinosaur gave him a ride away from the tracks. Then they played with the mother triceratops.

"You did it, Rubble!" exclaimed the engineer. "You saved the day!"

Meanwhile, Marshall found one of the baby pterodactyls in a tree. He wanted to return it to its mother. Marshall climbed up his fire ladder—and the dino bonked him with its beak! Marshall fell to the ground.

"I'm good!" Marshall said as the baby flapped down and landed gently on his tummy.

Skye arrived in her helicopter and lowered a harness to Marshall. He slipped into it, and as he was carried into the air, he called to the baby pterodactyl, "Follow me!"

The baby dinosaur flew all the way back to its nest with Marshall.

Over at the playground, Chase found another baby pterodactyl. He launched a net from his pack and snagged it.

Just then, the relieved mother pterodactyl flew down. She removed the net and happily took off with her baby.

Not far away, Skye zoomed over Adventure Bay and spotted the last baby pterodactyl. She swooped down to rescue it—and the giant Utahraptor jumped in her way!

"Keep your claws off that baby, you big bully!" Skye barked.

The giant raptor roared through Adventure Bay. It ate all the hamburgers, then swallowed all Mr. Porter's vegetables. It even gobbled up the PAW Patrol's favorite treats, liver links!

Watching this gave Rocky an idea.

A sausage link hit the raptor on the snout. Then another. And another!

Rocky had turned his truck into a sausage slinger. As it drove away from Adventure Bay, it flung links into the air. The Utahraptor followed, hungrily gulping down the treats.

"It's time to lead this parade out of town and into the jungle!" said Rocky.

The mother pterodactyl was glad to have her babies back.

"We were happy to help," says Ryder. "Whenever you're in trouble, just squawk for help."

Skye and Marshall took to the air, ready to lead the family to the jungle.

"*Aww*, you guys are going, too?" asked Rubble. The mother and baby triceratops roared goodbye as they lumbered away.

"They'll all be much happier in the jungle," said Ryder.

"Saving dinosaurs sure makes me tired," Rubble said with a yawn, and he stretched out on the grass. . . .

"Wake up, Rubble!" said Cap'n Turbot. "Nifty news! Those eggs you found are from a new species no one's ever seen! I named it Rubble-o-saurus!"

"Wow! Thanks!" said Rubble. He couldn't believe a dinosaur was now named after him. It was a dream come true!